Sydney's BIG Speech

To the history maker,
Alderman Edith "Edie" Newsome.
And to Ms. Director and Ms. Admiral,
you have no limits.—M.N.

For all the kids afraid
to let their words fly free.
(You got this!)—J.O.

Sydney's Big Speech

For information address HarperCollins Children's Books, a division of HarperCollins Publishers, 195 Broadway, New York, NY 10007.
www.harpercollinschildrens.com

Library of Congress Control Number: 2023937114
ISBN 978-0-06-314141-4

The artist used watercolor and digital media to create the illustrations for this book.
Designed by Elaine Lopez
23 24 25 26 27 RTLO 10 9 8 7 6 5 4 3 2 1

First Edition

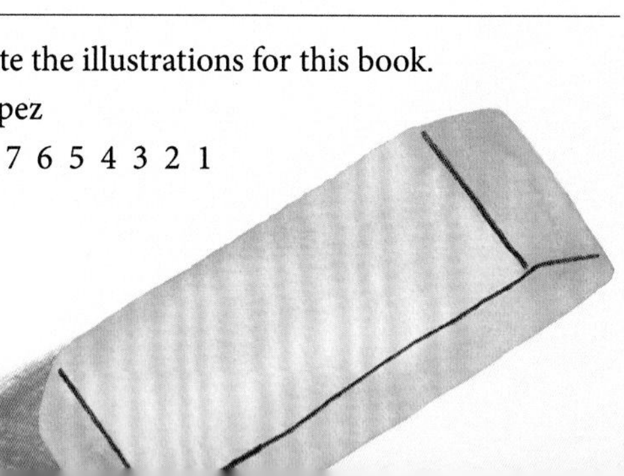

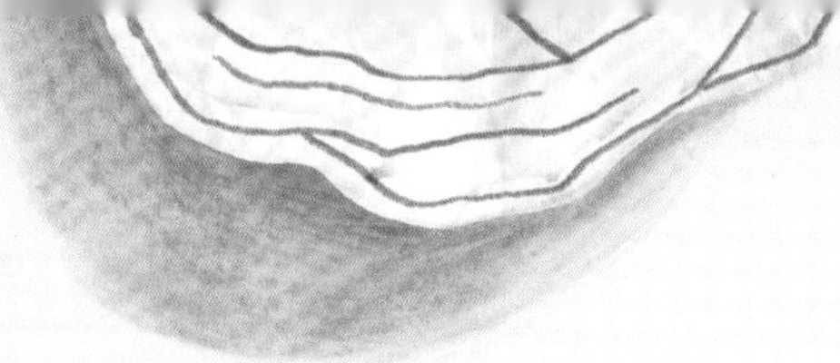

Sydney's BIG Speech

words by MALCOLM NEWSOME
art by JADE ORLANDO

HARPER
An Imprint of HarperCollinsPublishers

"Happy first day of school!" said Mr. Simmons.
"When I say your name, please stand and tell us something that you enjoy."

Sydney went last.
And when she stood, she kept her eyes toward the floor.

A million thoughts flooded Sydney's mind . . .

. . . but none of them found their way to her mouth.

So Sydney said nothing.
Nothing at all.

She plopped down and hung her head.
“Don’t worry, Sydney,” Mr. Simmons whispered. “You’ll have another chance.”

Then he made a big announcement.

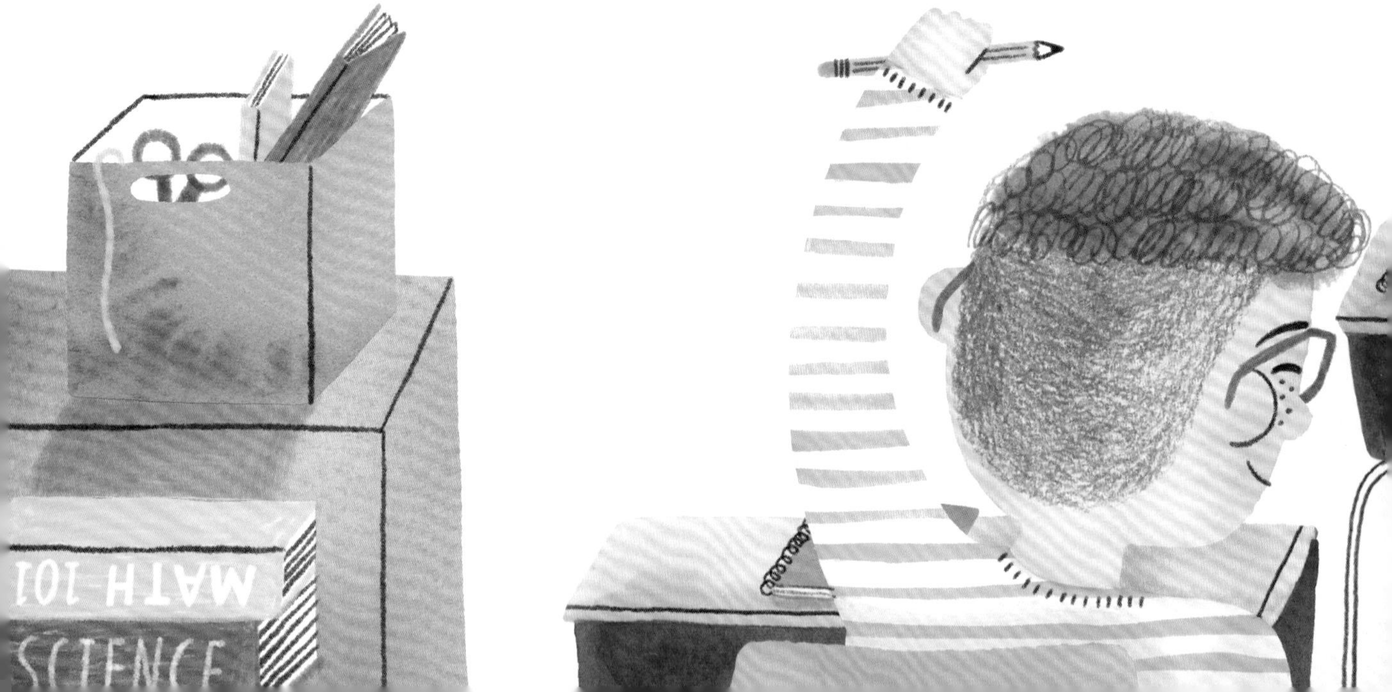

“Our first unit will be ‘When I Grow Up.’
At the end, everyone will give a speech to the class.”

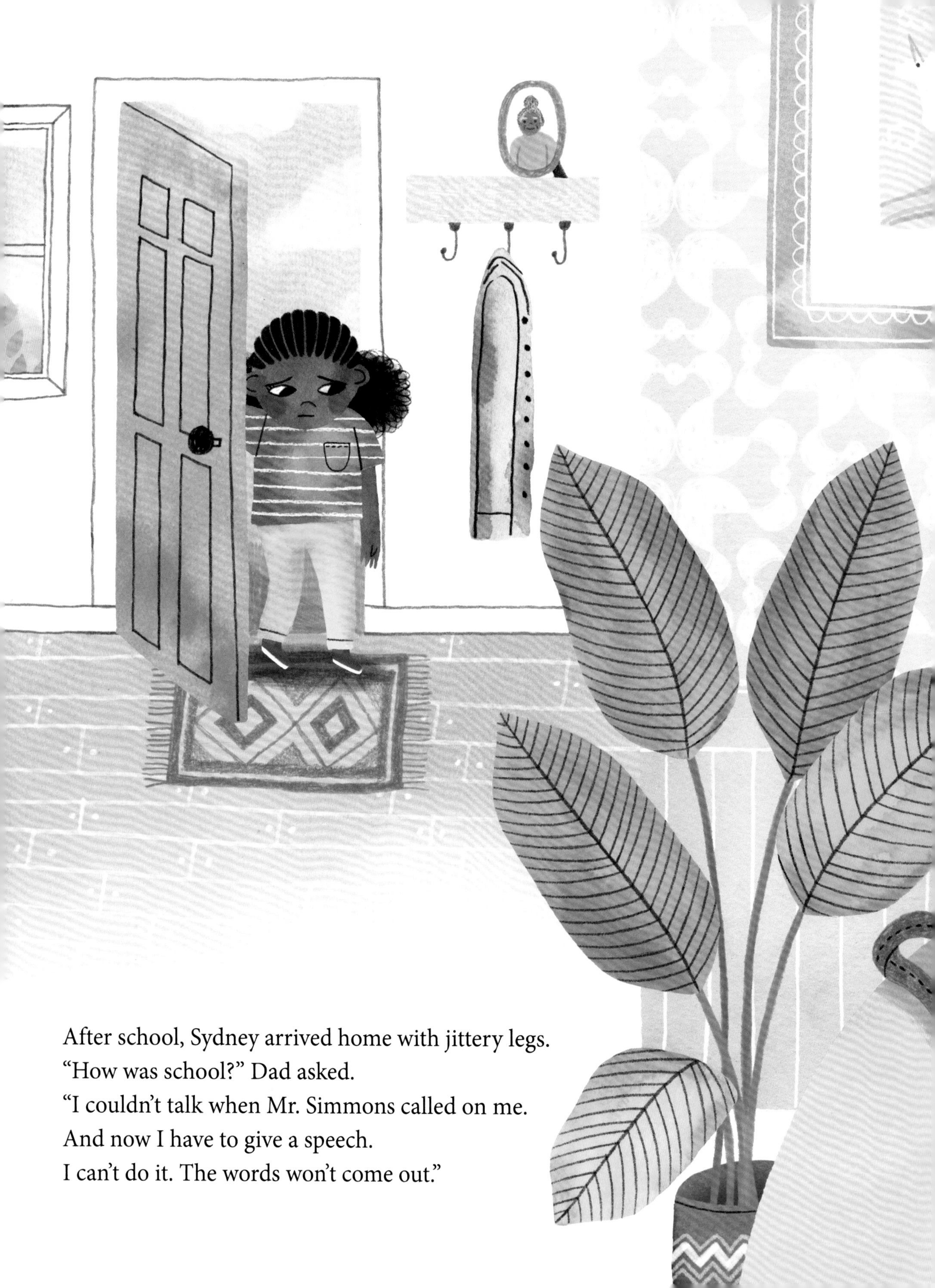

After school, Sydney arrived home with jittery legs.
"How was school?" Dad asked.
"I couldn't talk when Mr. Simmons called on me.
And now I have to give a speech.
I can't do it. The words won't come out."

KIND IS COOL

“I see,” her dad said. “I have an idea.
May I show you something?”

“This is Kamala Harris,
our first woman vice president.”

“DREAM with AMBITION,
lead with CONVICTION,
and see YOURSELVES in a
that others may not...”
“DREAM WITH AMBITION”

“Like you, she has lots of great words inside.
She just found a way to let the great words out.”

Afterward, he told her about . . .

Condoleezza Rice,
the first Black woman secretary of state,

Carol Moseley Braun,
the first Black woman senator,

and Shirley Chisholm,
the first Black woman to run
for president for a major party.

"I want to be a great leader like them when I grow up," Sydney said.
"You can," replied her dad.
"But great leaders have to give speeches. I'm bad at speeches."
"They had to *learn* how. And guess what?"
"What?"
"Since I'm shy, I had to learn, too. It just takes lots and lots of practice."

That night, Sydney sat in her thinking chair and made a plan.

First she and her dad watched video upon video of the other leaders' speeches.

Then she began practicing.

Each morning she practiced using wise words like Condoleezza Rice did.

At dinner she practiced using energetic words like Carol Moseley Braun did.

Before bed she practiced using powerful words like Shirley Chisholm did.

And, before long, she was using great words everywhere she went . . .

while watering
the flower garden,

in the grocery store,

and at the park.

But the night before her big speech, when Sydney stood alone in front of the mirror, she froze.

"What if I can't do this?" Sydney asked.

Sydney's dad knocked and stepped in.
"Hey, my little leader, I have something just for you."
Sydney tore open the wrapping to find the most perfect snow globe inside.

"And I have something else to share with you.
A speech that helps me when I'm feeling nervous."
He turned on a victory speech by his favorite president.

As Sydney watched, she saw the president speaking with ease. Near the end of the speech, the president repeated the words

Yes we can!

Yes we CAN!

And Sydney shouted,

Yes I CAN!

The next morning came sooner than Sydney wanted.
She stood alone at the front of the class.
Mr. Simmons asked, "What would you like to be when you grow up?"

Sydney raised her eyes.
She remembered Kamala Harris's hopeful words,
took a deep breath . . .

. . . and began.

When I grow up, I will dream big things and do big things. I will be a great leader who helps people and becomes the President!

“Well done, Sydney!” Mr. Simmons said.

When the student next to Sydney was called,
she saw him drop his head and freeze.
She leaned over and whispered in the boy’s ear . . .

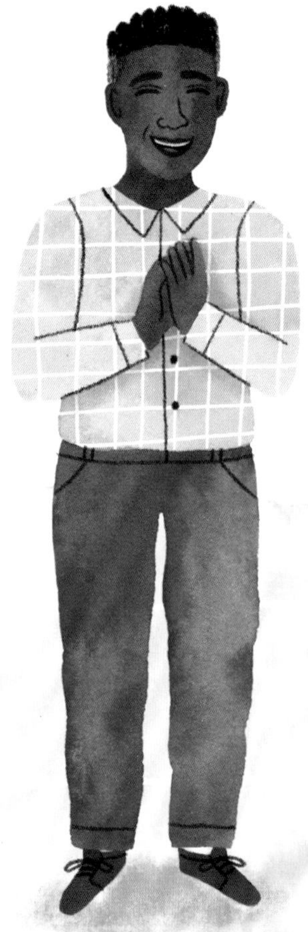

"Just let the great words out."

SHIRLEY CHISHOLM

First Black woman elected to the United States Congress (1969–83)

First Black woman to run for president of the United States for a major party (1972)

Quote: "We must reject not only the stereotypes that others have of us but also those that we have of ourselves and others."

Shirley Chisholm spoke with a lisp. When she was asked how she overcame that, she once said, "I'm not conscious of it . . . If you pay a lot of attention to it, it could give you hang-ups." Instead, she chose to focus on her great qualities and use those qualities to serve others as a teacher and a politician.

CAROL MOSELEY BRAUN

First Black woman elected to the United States Senate (1993–99)

Quote: "I'm really quiet and shy . . . I just had to get this ferocious because of this job."

Carol Moseley Braun overcame her quietness to fight hard for what she believed in. In 1993, Moseley Braun was one of two women to wear pants onto the Senate floor in defiance of an old rule that forbade women from doing so. The dress code was amended soon after.

CONDOLEEZZA RICE

First Black woman secretary of state (2005–9)

Quote: "[Great leaders] see the world as it should be, not as it is."

Condoleezza Rice, a well-known introvert, had a strong and serious commitment to learning and education. That, combined with a core belief that she had no limits, helped her ascend to one of the most powerful positions in the United States government.

KAMALA HARRIS

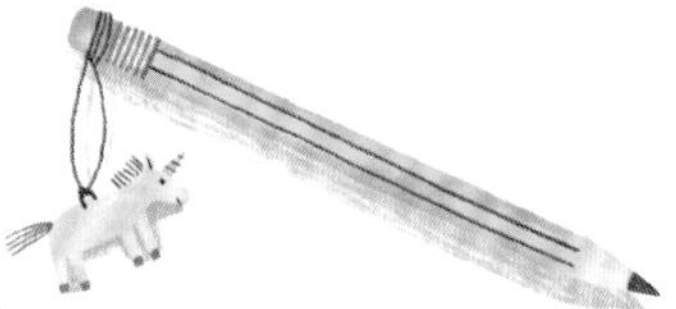

First woman vice president (2021–)

First Black and Asian American vice president (2021–)

Quote: "But while I may be the first woman in this office, I will not be the last. Because every little girl watching tonight sees that this is a country of possibilities."

Kamala Harris began finding her voice at an early age. At thirteen, she and her sister successfully protested a policy that banned kids from playing on the lawn of their apartment building.

References

Givhan, Robin. "Moseley Braun: Lady in Red." *Chicago Tribune*. January 21, 2004.

Kim, Catherine, and Zack Stanton. "55 Things You Need to Know About Kamala Harris." politico.com. August 11, 2020.

Lesher, Stephan. "The Short, Unhappy Life of Black Presidential Politics, 1972." *New York Times*. June 25, 1972.

Shogan, Robert. "Controversial Senator Pulls No Punches in Fight to Keep Seat." *Los Angeles Times*. August 17, 1998.

Winslow, Barbara. *Shirley Chisholm: Catalyst for Change*. Routledge. 2019.